A Strange Bird

by Stanford Makishi
illustration by Selina Alko

 HOUGHTON MIFFLIN   BOSTON

"Ugh! The summer's already over," Jason
said to himself. "I can't believe school starts
tomorrow." Jason lay on his back in a wide open
field, looking up at the dark clouds rolling in.

He glanced at his watch. It was time for dinner.
He stood up, stretched, and started walking home.
He went across the field and decided to take a
shortcut through the woods.

As Jason walked, he could hear the trees creaking
in the wind. A storm was coming in, and it was
getting dark. He knew that the rain would start
pouring down very soon.

Jason started walking faster and faster, until he was running. All of a sudden, he heard a loud snap behind him. As he ran, he turned to look back.

He didn't see the big log in front of him. His right foot hit the log, and he fell flat on his belly. "Ow!" he groaned. He felt a sharp pain in his left hand.

When Jason looked up, he saw a yellow bird standing right in front of his nose. It was a canary, and it seemed to be smiling at him. "What's a canary doing in the woods?" he wondered.

"I think I hurt my hand pretty bad," he said to the canary. The canary tilted its head, looked at Jason's hand, and hopped onto his palm. The canary started singing a sweet, beautiful song. Jason's hand seemed to hurt more, and he closed his eyes.

Suddenly, Jason felt the strange bird hop up onto his head. When he opened his eyes, he was stunned to discover that he was on the couch in his own living room!

"What am I doing here? My hand doesn't hurt anymore!" Jason shouted. He tried to look up at the canary who was still on his head. "Did you do that?" he asked.

"Jason, dear, why are you shouting?" Jason's mother was standing behind the couch, looking at her son. "And what is that bird doing on your head?"

Jason sat up and answered, "Mom, the most incredible thing just happened to me! I was running through the woods, and I fell down and hurt my hand, and this canary on my head brought me home *and* fixed my hand!"

His mother stared at him for a moment and said, "Jason, dear, that's impossible. You must have had a bad dream. Now please get that bird out of this house and wash up for dinner."

Jason looked at his mother and begged, "Mom, can I please keep the canary? It must have flown out of his cage. I'll just keep him until we find his owners. Please?"

She smiled. "Okay, dear, you can keep the canary until we find his owners. Go downstairs and get that old hamster cage. I think it's the right size. But you have to take care of this bird, okay?"

"I promise," said Jason. "I'll take excellent care of him. Just like he took care of me."

"Oh, Jason. You and those stories of yours," said Jason's mother as she walked into the kitchen.

"I'm not making this up," Jason said to himself. "I wasn't dreaming." Jason went downstairs to find the cage.

Jason looked around and saw the cage under a large stack of boxes. He went over to the cage, wrapped his arms around it, and pulled. Before he knew it, the boxes above him started to fall. "Oh, no!" Jason yelled, as one box after another tumbled on top of him. Soon he was trapped under a pile of boxes.

"Mom! Mom!" Jason yelled. Suddenly, the canary started to sing its sweet, beautiful song. Jason closed his eyes. He felt the bird hop up onto his head. "Here we go again," he said to himself.

When Jason opened his eyes, he was on the floor next to a neat stack of boxes. Beside the boxes was the hamster cage.

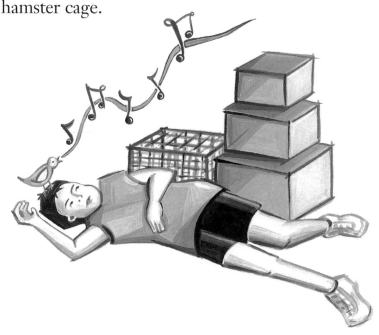

"Jason, did you call me? You know I'm very busy with this meatloaf," Jason's mom said from the top of the stairs.

"Mom, you're not going to believe this. I was trapped under this huge pile of boxes! And then the bird sang, saved me, and cleaned up the mess!"

"That's nice, dear," Jason's mother said. "You must be tired. Maybe you should just go to bed."

Jason took the cage to his bedroom. The canary stayed on Jason's head the whole time. Jason placed the cage in front of the window. Then he took from his pocket a piece of a branch he had broken off a tree earlier. He tied it to the sides of the cage. "That should make a good perch," he thought.

"How do you like it?" he asked the bird. The canary jumped off Jason's head, walked into the cage, and jumped up on the perch. He seemed to smile. "I think you like it," Jason said to the canary. He decided to keep the cage door open.

That night, as Jason was lying in bed, he thought about his strange day. "Maybe Mom was right. Maybe I was dreaming," he thought. Soon, Jason drifted off to sleep.

The next morning, Jason woke up to the sound of the school bus driving by his house. "Oh no! I can't believe it! I overslept on the first day of school," cried Jason.

He looked over at his alarm clock and saw that it was blinking. "The power must have gone off in the middle of the night. That's just great."

Jason put his face into his pillow. Suddenly, he heard the sweet, beautiful song of the canary. Then he felt the bird hop up onto his head.

When Jason lifted his head up and opened his eyes, he discovered that he wasn't in his bed anymore. He was in his classroom at school. He was dressed in his school clothes. Jason's friend Andrew was sitting next to him. "What is going on?" asked Jason.

"First day of school," Andrew answered. "What does it look like? And what are you doing with a canary on your head?"

"You wouldn't believe me if I told you," Jason replied.